GERONIMO
STILTON

Published by Sweet Cherry Publishing Limited
Unit 36, Vulcan House,
Vulcan Road,
Leicester, LE5 3EF,
United Kingdom

First published in the UK in 2018
2018 edition

ISBN: 978-1-78226-368-5

Text by Geronimo Stilton
Art Director: Iacopo Bruno
Graphic Designer: Laura Dal Maso / theWorldofDOT
Original cover illustration by Roberto Ronchi and Mirka Andolfo, Studio Parlapà
Concept of illustration by Gògo Gó in collaboration with Certosina Kashmir,
produced by Lorenzo Chiavini, Roberto Ronchi and Chiara Sacchi
Initial and final page illustrations by Roberto Ronchi and Ennio Bufi MAD5, Studio Parlapà and
Andrea Cavallini. Map illustrations by Andrea Da Rold and Andrea Cavallini
Cover layout and typography by Elena Distefano
Interior layout and typography by Rhiannon Izard and Amy Wong
Graphics by Michela Battaglin
© 2005 Edizioni Piemme S.p.A., Palazzo Mondadori – Via Mondadori, 1 – 20090 Segrate
© 2018 English edition, Sweet Cherry Publishing
International Rights © Atlantyca S.p.A. – via Leopardi 8, 20123 Milano, Italy
Translation © 2006 by Edizioni Piemme S.p.A.

Original title: *In campeggio alle cascate del Niagara*
Based on an original idea by Elisabetta Dami

www.geronimostilton.com/uk

www.sweetcherrypublishing.com

Printed and bound in Turkey

Geronimo Stilton

SCHOOL TRIP TO NIAGARA FALLS

Sweet Cherry
Publishing

OH, HOW I HATE BEING LATE!

"Rain, rain, go away." It was the middle of the night. I was in my **comfy, cosy bed**, trying to sleep. But the rain was beating on my window like a crazed woodpecker.

I fell asleep dreaming about birds and pounding ocean waves and huge crashing **WATERFALLS**. It rained the whole night. The next morning, I woke up

exhausted. I stared at the clock on my bedside table. **HOLEY CHEESE!** I was late! Oh, how I hate being late!

I hurled myself into the bathroom. I turned on the shower while brushing my teeth. I combed my whiskers while pulling on my trousers. I chugged down my coffee while racing out the door. Rats!

I ran at **BREAKNECK SPEED** to my aunt Sweetfur's house. That is where my little nephew Benjamin lives. I had promised to take him to school today.

Benjamin giggled when he saw me. I had forgotten to button my trousers. And my fur was sticking up **ALL OVER THE PLACE**.

On the way to school, we passed by my office. I run the most famous daily newspaper on Mouse Island. It is called The Rodent's Gazette.

Benjamin tugged on my paw. "Uncle, may I take my friends to visit you at the *Gazette* sometime?" he asked.

I smiled. My nephew was such a sweet and smart little mouse. Maybe someday he would follow in my pawsteps and run a newspaper too.

"Of course, dear nephew," I said. Finally, we arrived at Benjamin's school. **WHAT A ZOO!** Little rodents were running everywhere. Some held on to their parents' paws. Others tumbled off the school bus. Some zipped up on bicycles.

It was so loud I could barely hear myself squeak.

Just then, the school bell rang.

I nearly jumped out of my fur.

RRRRRIIIIINNNNNNNGGGG!

And that was when I spotted a blonde rodent. No, she wasn't just any blonde rodent. She had gorgeous fur. She had a sweet smile. And she had blue eyes the colour of a **CLEAR SUMMER SKY**.

"Good morning. I am Miss Angel Paws, Benjamin's teacher," she said.

I took a step towards her. But before I could shake her paw, I tripped over my tail. **I landed snout first in the dirt.**

DON'T WORRY ABOUT A THING!

I turned to run away with my tail between my legs. I was so **embarrassed**. Why did I have to make a fool of myself in front of such a *pretty* mouse?

"Today, we'll decide where to go on our school trip," I heard Miss Angel Paws announce.

Hmm. School trip. Suddenly, I had an idea. Maybe the class could come visit me at The Rodent's Gazette. Then the teacher would see I wasn't just a **clumsy, dim-witted mouse**. I strode back into the classroom.

"Oh, good, Mr. Stilton, you haven't left. I wanted to ask for your advice," Miss Angel Paws squeaked. "Do you think this is a good place to go on a school trip?"

She began writing something on the blackboard. I would love to tell you what it said, but I couldn't read it. No, it wasn't written in **ANCIENT SQUEAKEEZE**. I just couldn't see a thing. That's because the class bully Punk Rat had **tripped** me on my way in. I had lost my glasses.

The teacher tapped on the board. "What do you think, Mr. Stilton?" she repeated.

I squinted desperately at the board. I felt like one of the **three blind mice**.

Everything looked foggy. Then I thought of something. Maybe Miss Angel Paws wanted to visit The Rodent's

13

Gazette. Maybe that's what she had written on the board. Yes, that had to be it, I decided. That's why she wanted my advice.

"I think that's a great idea!" I said to the teacher. "I would love to take you there!"

Miss Angel Paws was amazed. "Really, Mr. Stilton?" she squeaked.

"Of course," I said. "And don't call me Mr. Stilton ... Call me **GERONIMO**!"

"But who will pay for it? When can we go? Don't you have to work?" asked the teacher.

"Don't worry about a thing," I told her. "I can take a little time off. You will all be my guests. We can go today if you'd like."

The teacher squealed with delight. She clapped her paws together. "Guess what, class? Mr. Stilton – I mean Geronimo – has volunteered to take all of us to **NIAGARA FALLS** for a whole week!" she announced. "We'll leave today!"

The class cheered.

"Hooray! We're going to **NIAGARA FALLS**! Thank you, Mr. Stilton!" they cried.

I blinked.

"Niagara Falls?'

Punk Rat pulled at one of my whiskers.

"Of course. Can't you read? Look at the blackboard," he smirked, handing me my glasses. I put them on. I stared at the blackboard. It read: **CLASS TRIP TO NIAGARA FALLS**.

I gulped. Oh, how did I get myself into such a mess?

The teacher was already calling the travel agency. "Yes, twenty-two students, a teacher, and Geronimo Stilton. We need twenty-four round-trip tickets to **NIAGARA FALLS**," she squeaked into the phone.

What could I do? The class was so excited they could hardly sit still.

With a sigh, I took out my credit card. It's a TOP MOUSE DIAMOND-PLUS-SUPER-DELUXE-EXTRA-SUPREME-GOLD CARD. It was a good thing I had it. This trip was going to cost me more than my two-year subscription to the Cheese of the Month Club!

TOP MOUSE
DIAMOND-PLUS-SUPER-DELUXE-EXTRA-SUPREME-GOLD CARD
Geronimo Stilton

After booking our trip, the teacher waved a yellow notebook in the air.

"Class, this notebook will be our travel journal," she announced. "We will write in it every day. **That way, we will never forget this wonderful trip.**"

17

THIS IS HOW TO KEEP A TRAVEL JOURNAL:

Today is: ....

We plan to visit: ....

The weather is:

We saw: ....

....

We really enjoyed: ....

....

....

 We ate: ....

....

We learned: ....
....
....
Surprises: ....
....

STICK A PHOTO OF
THIS DAY HERE!

This photo was taken at:...............................
....

ARE WE THERE YET?

Do you know how to get to **NIAGARA FALLS**? Let me tell you. The falls are located at the border of the United States and Canada. They are very far from Mouse Island. The flight was the longest one of my life. Well, OK, maybe it wasn't the longest, but it was *the worst*. That's because ...

Scampers spilled orange juice on my laptop.

Sakura smeared ice cream on my tie.

David pulled out one of my whiskers.

SCAMPERS SPILLED ORANGE JUICE ON MY LAPTOP ...

SAKURA SMEARED ICE CREAM ON MY TIE ...

DAVID PULLED OUT ONE OF MY WHISKERS ...

20

Carmen knocked down my suitcase.

Esmeralda squeaked my ear off.

Tim asked me 317 times, **"ARE WE THERE YET?"**

The whole time I tried desperately to read my book on **NIAGARA FALLS**.

NIAGARA FALLS

Located at the border of the United States (on the east) and Canada (on the west), the falls are formed by the waters of the Niagara River. During the journey from Lake Erie and Lake Ontario, the river suddenly drops more than 180 feet to the level of the riverbed, forming falls unique in their power.

There are actually two different falls at Niagara. On the Canadian side there is Horseshoe Falls, which is approximately 2,500 feet wide, while Rainbow Falls, on the American side, is approximately 1,000 feet in width.

In the winter, the river freezes, but the falls do not because they are in continuous movement.

Every second, more than 790,000 gallons of water fall!

Niagara Falls is also a precious source of electrical energy. Approximately 50 percent of the water (at night, 75 percent) is directed to the hydroelectric power plants that

ARCTIC OCEAN

NORTH
AMERICA

NIAGARA
FALLS

GULF OF
MEXICO

ATLANTIC OCEAN

PACIFIC OCEAN

SOUTH
AMERICA

supply the United
States and Canada
with electricity.

But the power of the
water is creating a problem
for the future of the falls. In the
past 12,000 years, the water
running over the rocks has
eroded them and shifted the
falls by almost seven miles.

A BIT OF HISTORY ...

THE ERA OF EXPLORATION

For centuries, only the Native Americans who lived at what is now the border between the United States and Canada knew about the spectacular falls. The first official news of their existence dates back to the second half of the sixteenth century. The man who made them famous was Louis Hennepin, a Belgian monk who was part of an expedition organised by the French explorer René-Robert Cavelier, Sieur de La Salle. The expedition arrived at the falls in December 1678, and its members were mesmerised by their size and grandeur.

At that time, the falls had a drop in level of more than 590 feet and carried twice as much water as they do now.

THE FIRST TOURISTS

Tourism was slow to arrive. One of the first important visits occurred in 1791, when the Duke of Kent (father of the future Queen Victoria of England) stayed at the only building in the area: a small wooden hut!

The first groups of tourists began arriving during the mid-1800s. The falls continued to attract important guests, such as Jerome Bonaparte, brother of the famous Napoleon. He came from New Orleans on his honeymoon. From that moment on, Niagara Falls became a popular destination for couples on their honeymoon.

EVERYONE EXCEPT ME!

Just before our plane landed, the captain made an announcement.

"Attention, rodents: we are now passing over the famouse **NIAGARA FALLS**. Take a look out of your window if you would like to see a truly *spectacular* view of the falls," he advised.

Everyone wanted to see the falls.

Everyone leaped to the window.

Everyone saw the spectacular view.

EXCEPT ME!

I was being suffocated by a throng of **SCREAMING, JUMPING MOUSELETS**. They had pressed themselves up against my window. I couldn't move. I couldn't breathe. I couldn't see a thing!

Finally, the plane landed. We were in Toronto, Canada. From there, we climbed on a bus. We rode on the bus for about an hour and a half. Then we arrived at the falls.

As we pulled up, the driver made an announcement. "We have now reached the famouse **NIAGARA FALLS**.

Look out of your window if you would like to see a truly spectacular view of the falls," he said.

Everyone wanted to see the falls.

Everyone leaped to the window.

Everyone saw the spectacular view.

EXCEPT ME!

A throng of **SCREAMING MOUSELETS** was crawling all over me. They plastered themselves up against my window. I couldn't move. I couldn't breathe. I couldn't see a thing!

The bus stopped. I got off.

The roaring sound of the falls was incredible.

I tried to take a picture.

Everyone wanted to take a picture of the falls.

Everyone got his or her camera ready.

Everyone snapped away at the falls.

28

EXCEPT ME!

Oh, if only I could get away from those **SCREAMING MOUSELETS**. They were all over me! I couldn't move. I couldn't breathe.

I couldn't see a thing!

The bus took us to the city of **NIAGARA FALLS** on the lake. **It was already dark.**

I Do Not Know How to Set Up a Tent!

WHAT A DAY! I was tired. I was hungry.

I stumbled off the bus. I couldn't wait to sink into a nice soft bed. I couldn't wait to put on my FLUFFY CAT-FUR SLIPPERS. I couldn't wait to order from room service.

"Is the hotel nearby?" I yawned. "I'm shattered."

Miss Angel Paws looked shocked.

"Hotel? Why, Mr. Geronimo, we have come to enjoy the great outdoors. We're not going to a hotel. We're going to camp out," she squeaked.

My eyes opened wide. I looked around. Miss Angel Paws wasn't joking. We were standing in the middle of the wilderness!

Did I mention I'm not much of an outdoor mouse?

"Um, yes, well, who's going to set up the tents?"

I stammered.

Miss Angel Paws rolled her eyes.

"You are, of course, Mr. Geronimo," she said.

I made a **QUICK** calculation: there were twenty-four of us. Each tent would hold four mice. That meant I had to set up six tents for the little mice. Then we would need one tent for me and one for Miss Angel Paws. Plus, we needed one big tent for all of us to eat breakfast in.

HOLEY CHEESE! I couldn't set up nine tents!

Just then, the little mice began whining. "Come on! We're tired!"

I couldn't make heads or tails of the tents.

I set up one tent inside out. I zipped myself up in another and couldn't get out. Then I whacked my paw with a hammer.

"I give up!" I screeched.

Did I mention I'm not much of an outdoor mouse? I sat down on a rock. I took off my glasses so I could sob freely. "Help! I can't do this!"

Just then, my little nephew Benjamin whispered in my ear.

I DO NOT KNOW HOW TO SET UP A TENT!

HERE GOES NOTHING

THIS GOES HERE ...

YIKES!

OR DOES IT GO THERE?

OUUUUUUCH!

HELP! GET ME OUT!

"Call Aunt Thea. She always knows what to do," he suggested.

I dried my tears. "Good idea," I agreed. I guess you could say my sister Thea is the opposite of me. She *loves* a challenge.

Half an hour later, after I talked to Thea on the phone, all of the tents were ready.

"Hooray!" yelled the little mice.

"Isn't it great sleeping in a tent, Mr. Geronimo?" Miss Angel Paws said.

THE TENT

HOW TO SET UP A TENT

1.

LAY THE TENT FLAT AND STAKE THE CORNERS.

2.

ASSEMBLE THE FRAME BY CONNECTING THE POLES, AND HOOK THE TENT TO THE FRAME.

3.

PULL THE LATERAL ROPES AND STABILISE THE TENT BY STAKING THE ROPES.

4.

MOUNT THE RAIN TARP AND ATTACH IT WELL WITH THE STAKES.

5.

Drainage ditch for water run-off

DIG A DRAINAGE DITCH AROUND THE TENT. YOU'LL NEED IT IN CASE OF RAIN.

WHERE TO SET UP A TENT

CHOOSE A FLAT AREA OR ONE ON A GENTLE SLOPE THAT IS WELL PROTECTED FROM THE WIND.

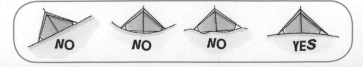

NO   NO   NO   YES

I Do Not Know How to Cook at a Campsite!

I was so tired I could only nod. Then I heard a low grumble. Was it a bear? Was it a fox? Was it a **RAVENOUS, RODENT-EATING MONSTER**? No, it was just my tummy. I was starving!

"So, who will do the cooking?" I asked.

"Why, you will, of course, Mr. Geronimo," Miss Angel Paws said.

The little mice began screaming.

"Come on! We're starving!" they whined.

I sighed. I trudged to the brook to get some water. But on the way back, I tripped. The water flew out of the bucket.

I decided to get the fire started. But the wood was too damp. It would not light.

I went to get some more wood and accidentally stepped on the egg carton. **CRUNCH!**

Then I noticed an army of ants. They were devouring all of the bread.

"I give up!" I squeaked. **Did I mention I'm not much of an outdoor mouse?**

"Try calling Aunt Thea again," Benjamin whispered. "She'll know what to do."

Half an hour later, the fire was ready.

Now if I could just get the ants off the bread ...

THE FIRE

HOW TO COOK OUTDOORS

TRIPODS

Bind three wooden poles together. Then hang a pot on a chain that has been secured at the top of the poles.

Arrange two forked sticks across from each other on either side of the fire. Hang the pots on a strong piece of wood, and then place each end of the wood in the forks.

FLAT ROCKS

Arrange several clean, flat rocks so they are heated by a fire underneath. You can cook eggs, fish, or meat on top of them.

FORKS

Before you light a fire, find out the wind's direction. Always be aware of the danger of fires! Keep a bucket of water nearby to put out the fire and always get help from an adult.

NEVER LEAVE FIRES UNATTENDED!

COME ON! WE HAVE TO GO!

After we ate, I fell asleep with my snout in my plate. I woke up with a start.

"Psst, psst, Mr. Geronimo!" a voice called.

It was Miss Angel Paws.

"Mr. Geronimo, you, um, forgot to set up a bathroom," she whispered.

I paled. A bathroom?

"Come on! We have to go!" the little mice squeaked.

This time, I knew exactly what to do. I called my sister. I wasn't proud. **I WAS DESPERATE.** After all, who knew how to set up a bathroom outdoors?

Of course, my sister figured it out. Half an hour later, the bathroom was finished. And so was I. I crawled into my sleeping bag and slept like a ten-ton brick of stale cheese. **Even a starving mouse couldn't have moved me.**

THE TOILET

HOW TO MAKE A BATHROOM

TOILET

1. DIG A HOLE. LEAVE A BIG PILE OF DIRT NEXT TO THE HOLE. AFTER EACH USE, THROW SOME PILED-UP DIRT INTO THE HOLE.

2. USE SOME WOODEN POLES AND A TARP TO BUILD A SCREEN AROUND THE TOILET.

SHOWER

SINK

3. BUILD A TRIPOD. HANG A BUCKET WITH WATER TO USE AS A MAKESHIFT SHOWER.

4. BUILD ANOTHER TRIPOD. PLACE A BOWL ON TOP TO WASH YOUR PAWS AND SNOUT.

WHAT A STINK! WHAT A SMELL! WHAT A STENCH!

I woke up in the middle of the night. An awful STENCH surrounded me. It smelled worse than my cousin Trap's rancid fish soup. It smelled worse than my grandmother Onewhisker's disgusting Brussels sprout soufflé.

I opened my eyes. A black and white furry creature with two beady little eyes stared back at me.

I jumped out of the sleeping bag, squeaking at the top of my lungs.

Torches snapped on all over the campsite.

"What a stink!"

"What a smell!"

"What a stench!" I heard the other campers cry.

40

I couldn't have agreed more. I started to chime in when I heard some more voices.

"Where is it coming from?" one said.

"That tent there," another answered.

"That's the rodent from New Mouse City. The one named **GERONIMO STILTON**," a third cried.

"He really needs to clean up his act," someone else piped up.

"Yeah, I wonder if he knows what the word *bath* means," another muttered.

I turned beet red. How could they talk about me that way? I'm no sewer mouse. I *love* taking baths.

But there was no time to think about a bubble bath now. I had to defend myself. "I'm not the stinky one," I started to explain. "It was that creature. It had black fur with a white stripe ..."

Punk Rat snickered. "What creature? I don't see any creature," he smirked.

Then he began to sing in a high-

PUNK RAT

pitched voice: "Geronimo sees things in the dark. A slug, a squirrel, a **giant shark**!"

Benjamin grabbed my paw. "Uncle, did you really see a creature?" he whispered. When I nodded, he stuck his snout in the tourist guide. I guess he was pretending he didn't know me. I couldn't blame him. **Everyone thought I was losing my whiskers.**

At that moment, Benjamin began squeaking. He held up the book. It showed a picture of the creature.

"See, my uncle was right!" my nephew told Punk Rat. **"The creature he saw is called a skunk!"**

A skunk is a mammal in the weasel family. It has a thick black coat with white stripes. It lives in woody areas and feeds on insects, small mammals, and fruit. To protect itself from predators, it uses a unique system: it raises its tail, spreads its hind feet, and sprays a smelly liquid that it can send as far as twelve feet.

A WALL OF RUSHING WATER

The next morning, we woke up at dawn.

After breakfast, we hiked along the river.

I was tired. You probably already know that I am not a morning mouse. But I was also excited. Finally, I would be able to see NIAGARA FALLS!

Our paws crunched through the thick autumn leaves of yellow, red, and brown. The air smelled crisp and fresh. Don't you just love autumn? I do. **I love everything about it.** Oh, except for Halloween. I'm not big on scary holidays.

I started thinking about the Halloween party my cousin Trap was throwing this year. He said he was going to dig up a real SKELETON and serve frozen eyeballs for dessert!

Just then, I felt like my own

...A MAGNIFICENT

eyeballs had **FROZEN**. Well, my eyeballs and the rest of my body, that is. I was staring at a tremendous wall of rushing water. We had reached the falls! The river rumbled like *THUNDER*. A magnificent rainbow made a bridge over the falls.

RAINBOW ...

Ah, what an unbelievable sight! I could have stood and admired the falls all day. I just had one little problem: the rushing water was getting to me. With a squeak, I took off in search of a bathroom.

NATIVE AMERICANS

NORTH-EAST

Algonquin: A community with lands in the Ottawa River valley.

Iroquois: A large confederation of communities, including the Cayuga, Mohawk, Oneida, Onondaga, Seneca, and Tuscarora. They have a matriarchal society: the chiefs are chosen by the clan's mother, the oldest and wisest woman.

Attawandaron: A non-warring community that lived on the shores of lakes Huron, Erie, and Ontario.

SOUTH-EAST

Cherokee: A community in Tennessee and North Carolina. A Cherokee leader, Sequoya, invented an alphabet for the Cherokee language that was made up of eighty-five symbols.

Creek: A confederation of communities from

Alabama, Georgia, and Florida.

Seminole: A community that immigrated to Florida and absorbed many runaway slaves.

SOUTH-WEST

Apache: A group of communities (Mescalero, San Carlos, Fort Apache, Apache Peaks, Mazatzal, and others) that share the same language. Famous chiefs include Geronimo and Cochise.

Navajo: Native people of northern New Mexico and Arizona, they are famous for their craftwork, including blankets, rugs, and jewellery.

Pueblo: A group of communities based around Arizona and New Mexico. This term also refers to the flat-roofed stone or adobe houses in which these Native Americans traditionally lived. Their houses were sometimes several storeys high.

PLAINS

Cheyenne: A community based in Montana and Oklahoma, the Cheyenne once lived in tepees made from long poles and buffalo skins. They were skilled buffalo hunters.

Comanche: A community based in Oklahoma, the Comanche originate from the Great Plains, where they were known as skilled horsemen.

Blackfoot: A community who now live in Montana and parts of Canada, the Blackfoot Nation were famous for their shoemaking ability. The Blackfoot dyed their moccasins black.

Sioux: A group of communities, also known as the Lakota. Sitting Bull, Crazy Horse, and Red Cloud are famous Sioux chiefs.

HIGHLANDS AND LOWLANDS

Nez Percé (or Pierced Noses): A peaceful community in Idaho, Washington, and Oregon. In the past, some of the population were known for wearing objects piercing their noses.

Shoshone: A community based in California, Idaho, Nevada, Utah, and Wyoming. The Shoshone were buffalo hunters who sought peace with the white population during the Indian Wars.

CALIFORNIA

Hoopa: A community of artisans who live in the Hoopa Valley. They are known for their use of acorns and salmon in their traditional meals.

Wintu: A community who live in California. Their economy was once based on deer, salmon, and acorns.

NORTH-WEST

Chinook: A community of famous salmon merchants on the north shore of the Columbia River in Oregon.

Tlingit: A community skilled in working cedar wood, who live on the islands and coast of Alaska.

ALL ABOARD!

A few minutes later, I was back at the falls. Miss Angel Paws was making an announcement.

"We will now board a boat called the ***Maid of the Mist*** that will take us to the falls," she told the class. "Please do not lean over the side."

We put on shiny raincoats. Then we climbed aboard the boat.

It sailed straight up the Niagara River. Everything looked so different from below.

A mist rose up from the **SPRAYING WATER**. We were so close to the falls.

I dug my paws into the railing of the deck. The water churned below us. I was glad we were all safe on the boat.

The sprays of water soaked my fur. Oh, well. No one could say I was STINKY now.

I looked around. We were surrounded by fog.

A VISIT TO THE FALLS

The experience on board the *Maid of the Mist* is a very damp one, since the ship, navigating through sprays, goes right to the base of the falls. It is a breathtaking trip, and one of the best ways to appreciate the strength of this enormous body of water.

I felt like I was in a dream.

Just then, I remembered a story that I had read about **NIAGARA FALLS**. I told it to the class.

A long, long time ago ...

The Legend
of the
Maid of the Mist

Many years ago, a community of Native Americans lived peacefully near the Niagara River. In order to protect themselves from disease and hunger, the community always asked the god of thunder, who lived in a cave under the falls, for protection.

One day, the god saw Lelawala, the daughter of the great chief Eagle Eye, and decided to keep her for himself. The Native Americans offered him canoes full of flowers, fruit and game, but the god insisted on marrying her. Lelawala was courageous and decided to protect her community by marrying the god. She showed up dressed in white, with a garland of flowers. She boarded a white birch canoe and bravely hurled herself over the falls. But when she fell from the top, the god stretched out his arms and saved her. The courageous young girl remained forever in the cave under the falls.

She was called the Maid of the Mist because at the base of the falls, there is always a dense mist made of droplets of water.

DON'T MOVE, PUNK RAT!

When I finished telling the story, I looked up. The boat was returning to shore. Right then, I noticed something. It was quiet. **TOO QUIET.** I began to get the feeling that something – or someone – was missing.

I ran up and down the boat counting the little mice. "One, two, three, four, five, six, seven, eight ..."

I was right. **We were short one rodent.**

Can you guess who was missing? Here's a hint: he's the loudest mouse in the class and a pain in my tail. That's right, it was Punk Rat.

Suddenly, I spotted the little pest on the shore. He must have been left behind when the boat took off.

"Don't move, Punk Rat!" I yelled.

"**IT'S DANGEROUS!** We'll come and pick you up."

But at that moment, disaster struck. Punk Rat slipped on a wet rock. **He tumbled into the water.**

HE DISAPPEARED INTO A MENACING WHIRLPOOL

A Dive ... in the Icy Water!

A little voice inside my head began screaming at me. "Don't just stand there! Save him!" it yelled. I dove into the water. That's when the other little voice began screaming. It shrieked, "Geronimo, are you crazy? You're not a swimmer. You can barely do two laps at the Cheddarville pool!"

ICY-COLD WATER soaked into my ears, my nose, even my throat. It blocked out the voices. All I could think about was saving Punk Rat.

I swam desperately towards him. I could see his little head bobbing up and down in the waves. His little paws waved in the air. Up and down, wave. Up and down, wave. He looked like he was doing a perfect water ballet dance. I wondered if he had ever thought about taking lessons.

I was still thinking about water ballet when things went from bad to worse. Yep, Punk Rat went under.

What could I do? I dove down after him.

It was dark under the water. I could hardly see a thing. Everything was so fuzzy. Everything was so blurry. *Maybe I need a new pair of glasses*, I thought. Then I realised I wasn't wearing glasses. I had lost them in the water!

Luckily, my paw felt something. It was Punk Rat's tail. I grabbed it. I pulled him up.

Someone threw me a life buoy from the boat. Then they pulled us in.

Cheesecake! We were saved!

You Are Not a Mouse ... You Are a Hero!

The boat's captain patted me on the back. "Nice going, Mr. Stilton!" he exclaimed. Then he led the crowd in a chorus of cheers.

"HiP, hiP, hooray! HiP, hiP, hooray!" they shouted.

A large, beefy tourist threw his paws around me. "That was beautiful," he squeaked. "Who would think a scraggly little rodent like you could do something like that?" He embraced me in a crunching hug. I felt all the **BONES** in my body snapping. Then he accidentally stepped on my foot.

"Oooooooooooooouuuuuch!" I screamed at the top of my lungs.

I quickly wrapped my foot in my nephew's bandanna.

Next, a little old lady mouse gave me a kiss. She had tears in her eyes.

"Bravo, young man! You are not a mouse ... You are a hero!" she exclaimed.

While she was kissing me, the handle of her purse went into my eye.

"Oooooooooooouuuuuch!" I screamed at the top of my lungs. My eye felt like it was on **FIRE**. I tied a handkerchief around my head to soak up the tears. Now I looked just like a pirate.

The whole class stared at me. I could tell they were impressed. Little mice love **pirates**.

"You're so lucky to have such a COOL UNCLE,"

Sakura told Benjamin.

My nephew beamed with pride.

Punk Rat and I were wet and shivering. A sailor wrapped us in a blanket. He gave us each a cup of hot chocolate.

My paws were shaking so much I spilled mine all over me. **"Oooooooouuuch!"** I screamed at the top of my lungs.

Oh, when would this day come to an end?

FRIENDS ... FUREVER!

When Punk Rat stopped shivering, he wrapped his paws around my neck.

"Thank you, Geronimo! You saved my life! I'm sorry I played all those dumb tricks on you," he gushed.

I tried to say something, but I couldn't squeak. I couldn't move. **I COULDN'T BREATHE.** Punk Rat was squeezing my neck so tightly I was choking!

At last, he let go. Then he shook my paw.

"Friends ... furever!" the little rodent squeaked.

I gave him a weak smile. **"Furever," I croaked, still gasping for breath.**

THE ADVENTURE SEEKERS
OF
NIAGARA FALLS

Many people have come to Niagara Falls seeking fame and adventure. Here are just a few of the most famouse.

The first daredevil was Jean-François Gravelet, known as Blondin. In 1859 and 1860, he crossed the falls by walking on a steel rope stretched across the top.

The first woman to hurl herself over the falls inside a wooden barrel was Annie Taylor, sixty-three years of age. She completed the feat in 1901, accompanied by her cat.

After his first attempt failed because the authorities stopped him, Dave Munday succeeded in hurling himself over the falls in a barrel twice, once in 1985 and once in 1993.

Bobby Leach faced the falls in 1911. He locked himself in a steel barrel, but he was less lucky than Annie. He was in the hospital for six months with various broken bones.

Isn't It Magnificent, Geronimo?

Before we got off the boat, Benjamin spotted something floating in the water. It was my glasses. I reached over the side to fish them out, and ... **splash!** I fell in.

I swam to shore. I was wet. I was cold. But I could see! I was in *mouse heaven*! I wondered if my glasses had missed me as much as I missed them.

We hiked back towards the camp.

We took a shortcut through the woods.

I looked around. The leaves on the trees were such *beautiful colours* – red, orange, brown, gold. If I were an artist, I would have painted a picture. But I'm not. In fact, I was the only mouselet at Little Tails Academy to ever fail paw painting.

I trudged along, breathing in the fresh, crisp air. I really am a **nature lover** at heart.

"Isn't it magnificent, Geronimo?" Miss Angel Paws said.

Benjamin and his friends were running ahead. At last, I was alone with the teacher. I decided now was my chance. I had to find out more about this **BEAUTIFUL MOUSE**. Maybe we could go out to dinner sometime. I wondered if she would like Le Squeakery. It's my favourite French restaurant.

"So, um, Miss Angel Paws," I began shyly. "Are you married?"

Miss Angel Paws shook her head. A big tear rolled down her fur. Then she collapsed in a fit of sobs.

Oh, why did I have such rotten luck with female mice? If they weren't crying, they were running away from me.

The teacher pulled herself together. "Sorry," she sniffed. "I am not married. But I was in *love* once, a long, long time ago ..."

Carefully, she opened a locket that she wore around her neck. Inside was a whisker.

"This is his whisker," Miss Angel Paws explained. "It is all I have left of him. The last time I saw him, he was being chased by an **ANGRY CAT**. I swore I

would never fall in love again."

I sighed. What a sad, sad story. I felt bad for the whiskerless mouse. I felt bad for Miss Angel Paws. Right then, it began to rain. **The water poured down in buckets.**

Miss Angel Paws's locket

LOVE UNDER A CHEESE-COLOURED UMBRELLA

Suddenly, a mouse appeared out of nowhere. He was carrying a large cheese-coloured umbrella.

"Please, allow me," he said softly to Miss Angel Paws. He held the umbrella over her head and smiled.

The two rodents stared at each other. They stared and stared. I wondered what the staring contest was all about. Then I noticed something. The mouse with the umbrella was missing a whisker. Could it be? I wondered.

Just then, the two mice clasped paws. **"It's you!"** they squeaked together.

Well, that answered that question. It was all pretty amazing. I mean, what were the chances Miss Angel Paws would find her lost love at **NIAGARA FALLS**? That's like finding a cheese cracker in

an overflowing RUBBISH BIN. It takes more than just digging. It takes luck!

I was happy for the teacher. At least someone was having a lucky day. I, on the other paw, was not. The rain seeped into my fur. It dribbled down my whiskers. It poured into my ears. I was getting **SOAKED**. I could see the little mice huddled together in a dry cave up ahead.

Meanwhile, the two love mice had the cheese-coloured umbrella to protect them. Not that they seemed to notice it was raining. They looked like they were under some kind of *magic spell*. The kind that

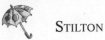

makes you forget where you are.

I sighed. I wished I were under a magic spell. **Then I could forget I was standing outside in the middle of a torrential rainstorm!**

A REAL GENTLE MOUSE

That night, we sat around a **CRACKLING CAMPFIRE**. It turned out Miss Angel Paws's friend was a forest ranger. His name was Gentle Mouse. I wanted not to like him. After all, I came on this trip just to spend more time with Miss Angel Paws. But how could I hate a rodent with a name like that?

Gentle Mouse knew a lot about nature. He showed us a maple leaf.

"From this tree, we get maple syrup," Gentle Mouse explained. He told the class how they could start their own collection of dried leaves.

Maple Syrup

The sap from maple trees can be boiled down and made into maple sugar or maple syrup. When winter turned into spring, Native Americans would make V-shaped slashes in a maple tree trunk and collect the sap in a vessel. Then they would boil the sap down into sugar. The early European settlers learned this way of getting maple sugar from the Native Americans.

HOW TO MAKE A COLLECTION OF DRIED LEAVES

1 Gather some leaves that have fallen to the ground. Take care to choose the most beautiful ones - with lots of different colours, shapes, and dimensions.

2 As soon as you get home, clean the leaves well. To dry them, place them between two sheets of paper inside a thick book.

3 When the leaves are dry and flat, glue them in a notebook or put them in a photo album.

4 Next to each leaf, write its name and the date it was collected.

5 Near each leaf's common name, you can write its botanical name, which can be found in an encyclopedia or field guide.

Elm
(Ulmus americana)

American Beech
(Fagus grandifolia)

American Chestnut
(Castanea dentata)

Paper Birch
(Betula papyrifera)

CHEEP ... CHEEP ...
CHEEP ... CHEEP ...

The next morning, we went for a hike through the woods. I tried to keep up with the group, but I kept tripping over rocks and twigs. **Did I mention I'm not much of a sports mouse?**

Gentle Mouse pointed out the different plants along the way.

"This is a sugar maple. Its leaf is on the Canadian flag," he explained. "This is a chestnut tree. Has anyone ever tried a chestnut?"

Just then, I saw two beady eyes blinking behind the bushes. "Look, a fox," Gentle Mouse whispered excitedly.

I gulped. I was okay with plants, but wild animals weren't exactly my cup of Cheddar. They can be a little scary. No, make that **DOWNRIGHT TERRIFYING**!

I scampered past the fox. Gentle Mouse was busy pointing out other animals. We saw a beaver, a raccoon, and even a moose with **huge** antlers.

I couldn't believe how many wild animals we came across. Suddenly, I heard a loud chirping. Cheep! Cheep!

I followed the chirping to an oak tree. A little bird was lying on the ground.

"Help! It's fallen and it can't get up!" I told Gentle Mouse. **"What should we do?"**

SOS

HOW TO GIVE FIRST AID TO A BIRD

1. When you find a little bird fallen to the ground, call the RSPB. Then look for the bird's nest around that area. Leave the bird alone and wait a little while ... Its parents could come to claim it.

2. If there is no nest, pick the bird up from the ground gently.

3. If the bird is very small and still without feathers, you need to feed it, using a dropper.

4. If the bird has feathers, take a look at its beak. If it's short and strong, feed it grain seeds. If it's long and thin, feed it insects.

5. Keep the bird in a warm place that is similar to its nest, like a box with a woollen cloth.

6. As soon as the bird is able to fly, set it free. And remember, ask a parent or adult before touching any wild animal!

THE FOREST IS ON FIRE!

Gentle Mouse showed us how to make a nest using a box and a towel. We found some seeds and fed them to the bird. It let out a happy chirp. Then it started smoking. **HOLEY CHEESE!** What was in those seeds? Then I realised the smoke wasn't coming from the bird. It was filling the air around us!

"FIRE!" someone screamed.

Gentle Mouse called for help on his mobile phone. "Hurry! The forest is on fire!" he cried. "Someone must have left a campfire burning. Send a plane right away!"

Gentle Mouse told everyone to stay calm. He divided us up into two teams.

The first team dug fire trenches. "If we cut down all of the plants, the fire will have nothing to burn," Gentle Mouse explained.

The second team formed a long chain that ended at a nearby brook. The first mouse in line filled a pail with water. Then he passed it down the line. The last mouse in line threw the water on the flames.

We worked like pack rats, but the heat was becoming **UNBEARABLE**. My fur was scorched. The smoke was making me choke.

Suddenly, a miracle happened. We heard the sound of engines. It was a plane carrying an **enormouse** tank filled with water! The plane dumped the water onto the flames and then left to pick up more water from the lake. **WE WERE SAVED!** But before we could celebrate, Gentle Mouse began shouting. "Has anyone seen Miss Angel Paws?"

"I saw her running towards those bushes. I think she was trying to help a wounded fawn," Kay cried.

"Don't worry, Miss Angel Paws!" Gentle Mouse yelled. "I'll save you!"

He disappeared in a cloud of smoke. A few minutes

later, he returned. He was carrying the teacher in his paws. "*My hero,*" giggled Miss Angel Paws. "He saved the fawn, too!"

I felt a twinge of jealousy. Why couldn't I be someone's hero? **Still, I had to admit, Miss Angel Paws and Gentle Mouse were a match made in mouse heaven.**

Have I Got a Surprise for You!

That night, the two love mice made an announcement. Can you guess what it was?

Yes, they had decided to get married.

"Hooray!" cried the class. Everyone was so excited. But they were even more excited when they heard that Miss Angel Paws and Gentle Mouse wanted to get married immediately. They had been missing each other for years. They didn't want to wait any longer.

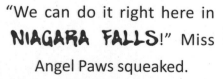

"We can do it right here in **NIAGARA FALLS**!" Miss Angel Paws squeaked.

We put our heads together to plan the ceremony. It would have to be pretty simple. There would be no wedding gown or fancy wedding cake. After all, where could we get a dress and a cake in the middle of the wilderness?

I called my sister to ask for her advice. As I said, that mouse just *loves* a challenge.

An hour later, my mobile phone **RANG**. It was Thea. "Hey, Gerry Berry, have I got a surprise for you!" she squeaked.

I gulped. A surprise? From my sister? The last time she surprised me, she carpeted my whole apartment in PINK CAT FUR!

FLAP, FLAP, FLAP ...
VROOOOOOMMMMM!

Right at that instant, I heard a strange noise over my head.

Flap, flap, flap ... **VROOOOMMM!**

Flap, flap, flap ... **VROOOOMMM!**

Flap, flap, flap ... **VROOOOMMM!**

I looked up and screamed.

A pink helicopter was circling above me.

Pink sugar-coated almonds rained down all around me.

Pink invitations with the bride's and groom's names on them flew through the air.

A bunch of thorny pink roses hit me in the snout. **Youch!**

So this was my sister's surprise. I was relieved. I'd take a thorn in the snout over that awful pink carpeting

any day.

I told everyone who the nutty mouse flying the plane was.

"My sister loves pink," I added.

At that moment, an enormouse pink package struck me on the head. Before I fainted, I noticed a note on the side of the box. It said:

For Angel Paws and Gentle Mouse

When I came to, the others were busy opening Thea's package. No one gave me a second glance. I snorted. **So much for mousely manners.** It was clear that all anyone cared about was the box.

What was inside? It was a full-

Pink almonds

Pink notes

Pink roses

length wedding dress and a tux. Now everyone was happy. Well, everyone except me, that is. A lump had formed on top of my head. **It was the size of a mega-huge ball of mozzarella!**

The Suprise
Package

Barbecue Time!

After the wedding ceremony, we headed back to the campsite. When we arrived we were overwhelmed by a delicious smell. I sniffed the air. Could it be? Yes, it smelled just like a **barbecue**.

I ran towards the campsite. That's when I spotted a big poster leaning against a rock. It said:

BARBECUE!
COME ONE, COME ALL.
GET READY FOR THE BEST BARBECUE
THIS SIDE OF NIAGARA FALLS!
BROUGHT TO YOU BY THE
BEST CHEF IN THE WORLD!

I scratched my fur. There was only one rodent I knew who was that full of himself. There was only one rodent I knew who was that irritating ... **such a pain!**

My cousin Trap!

Just then, a pair of whiskers emerged from behind a cloud of smoke. A pot-bellied rodent wearing a loud Hawaiian-print shirt stood behind a smoking grill. He waved a greasy spatula at me. "Yo, Germeister, what's squeaking?" he smirked. "Love the lump on your head. It's **SOOOOO** you!"

I rolled my eyes. Yep, it was my cousin Trap, all right. Have I mentioned he's a total pain in my tail?

I started to explain about the bump on my head when Trap interrupted me.

"Listen up, rodents!" he called. "You're about to taste the best cooking around. So don't drag your paws, it's time to eat. Now that you've found Trap, you can throw away your map. That's TRAP —

T as in LOOK OUT, TONGUE, YOU'RE IN FOR A TREAT!

R as in READY OR NOT, HERE IT COMES!

A as in ASK ME IF I CAN COOK.

P as in PAY ATTENTION, THE NAME IS TRAP!"

Yes, there is one thing you should know about my cousin. He's in *love*. No, not with another mouse. With himself!

Still, I had to admit his barbecue was delicious. I stuffed my snout like my uncle Cheesebelly at a make-your-own-cheese-sundae buffet.

After dessert, Thea took me on a helicopter ride over

Delicious! Yum Yum! Yum! Yum!

the falls. It really was a spectacular sight. Too bad I got sick on the way down. **I knew I shouldn't have eaten three pieces of cheesecake!**

Yum!

Yum!

Yum!

That hit the spot!

LITTLE MICE AROUND THE WORLD

Finally, it was time to go home. We boarded the plane headed for Mouse Island. It was another **long flight**. The little mice climbed all over me. Then they sang songs at the top of their lungs. I didn't get one bit of rest. Still, I was kind of sad when we landed. I was going to miss those little rodents.

As we were waiting for our luggage, I made an announcement. "You are all invited to visit me at The Rodent's Gazette," I told the class. "You can see how we put the newspaper together. You can see how a book is made."

"Hooray!" the little mice cheered.

Then Punk Rat grabbed my paw.

"I'm going to miss you, Mr. Geronimouse," he sobbed.

I patted his head.

"I'll miss you too, Punk Rat," I said. "Um, but remember, my name is Geronimo, *Geronimo Stilton*."

"Of course, Mr. Geronimity," Punk Rat squeaked.

I tried to remain calm. "It's Geronimo, Punk Rat," I repeated. "That's **G-E-R-O-N-I-M-O**."

Punk Rat smirked. "That's what I said, Mr. Geronimoose," he giggled.

I gave up. What else could I do?

Punk Rat flung his paws around my neck. He really

100

wasn't such a **BAD LITTLE MOUSE**. In fact, he was just like lots of little mice around the world – full of life and love and, oh, of course, **CHEESE**.

To Travel … Is Better Than to Arrive

We headed for the airport exit. A school bus was waiting for Miss Angel Paws and her class. I waved goodbye. "I'll take a taxi home," I told them.

A line of cheese-coloured taxis waited at the kerb. But for some reason, my paws didn't want to budge. My bag felt like **IT WEIGHED A TON**. An overwhelming feeling of sadness came over me. It had been such an exciting adventure. And now it was over.

Just then, I remembered a line from one of my favourite authors. His name was Robert Louis Squeakenson. Do you know him? He wrote a book called *Treasure Island*. Anyway, he said that **TO TRAVEL IS BETTER THAN TO ARRIVE**.

Well, I don't know if that is

R. L. Squeakenson

true all of the time. Usually, I am thrilled to get back to my comfy, cosy mouse hole. But this time, I still had the travel bug in me.

And so I did what any **smart mouse** would do. I turned around and headed right back into the airport.

I, Geronimo Stilton, booked a trip to Blue Cheese Island. I hear it's supposed to be beautiful there this time of year. Blue skies, blue waters, and lots and lots of blue cheese.

I couldn't wait to get there!

THE RODENT'S GAZETTE

1. Main entrance
2. Printing presses (where everything is printed)
3. Accounts department
4. Editorial room (where editors, illustrators, and designers work)
5. Geronimo Stilton's office
6. Geronimo's botanical garden

MAP OF NEW MOUSE CITY

MAP OF MOUSE ISLAND

1. Big Ice Lake
2. Frozen Fur Peak
3. Slipperyslopes Glacier
4. Coldcreeps Peak
5. Ratzikistan
6. Transratania
7. Mount Vamp
8. Roastedrat Volcano
9. Brimstone Lake
10. Poopedcat Pass
11. Stinko Peak
12. Dark Forest
13. Vain Vampires Valley
14. Goosebumps Gorge
15. The Shadow Line Pass
16. Penny-Pincher Castle
17. Nature Reserve Park
18. Las Ratayas Marinas
19. Fossil Forest
20. Lake Lake
21. Lake Lakelake
22. Lake Lakelakelake
23. Cheddar Crag
24. Cannycat Castle
25. Valley of the Giant Sequoia
26. Cheddar Springs
27. Sulphurous Swamp
28. Old Reliable Geyser
29. Vole Vale
30. Ravingrat Ravine
31. Gnat Marshes
32. Munster Highlands
33. Mousehara Desert
34. Oasis of the Sweaty Camel
35. Cabbagehead Hill
36. Rattytrap Jungle
37. Rio Mosquito
38. Mousefort Beach
39. San Mouscisco
40. Swissville
41. Cheddarton
42. Mouseport
43. New Mouse City
44. Pirate Ship of Cats

THE COLLECTION

HAVE YOU READ ALL OF GERONIMO'S ADVENTURES?

☐ *Lost Treasure of the Emerald Eye*

☐ *The Curse of the Cheese Pyramid*

☐ *Cat and Mouse in a Haunted House*

☐ *I'm Too Fond of My Fur!*

☐ *Four Mice Deep in the Jungle*

☐ *Paws Off, Cheddarface!*

☐ *Fangs and Feasts in Transratania*

☐ *Attack of the Pirate Cats*

ABOUT THE AUTHOR

Born in New Mouse City, Mouse Island, GERONIMO STILTON is Rattus Emeritus of Mousomorphic Literature and of Neo-Ratonic Comparative Philosophy. For the past twenty years, he has been running The Rodent's Gazette, New Mouse City's most widely read daily newspaper.

Stilton was awarded the Ratitzer Prize for his scoops on *The Curse of the Cheese Pyramid* and *The Search for Sunken Treasure*. He has also received the Andersen Prize

for Personality of the Year. His works have been published all over the globe.

In his spare time, Mr. Stilton collects antique cheese rinds and plays golf. But what he most enjoys is telling stories to his nephew Benjamin.